The Adventures of
Titch & Mitch

The Adventures of
Titch & Mitch

Book 3
The King of the Castle

Garth Edwards
Illustrated by Max Stasyuk

INSIDE
POCKET

Published in Great Britain by Inside Pocket Publishing Limited

First published in Great Britain in 2010

Text © Garth Edwards, 2009

The right of Garth Edwards to be identified as the author of this work has been asserted in accordance with the Copyright, Designs and Patents Act 1988.

Illustrations © Inside Pocket Publishing Limited

Titch and Mitch is a registered trade mark of Inside Pocket Publishing Limited

A CIP catalogue record for this book is available from the British Library

ISBN 978-0-9562315-2-9

Inside Pocket Publishing Limited Reg. No. 06580097

Printed and bounds in Great Britain by CPI Bookmarque Ltd, Croydon

www.insidepocket.co.uk

For N & J

Contents

Map of Island

Dragon Mouse Cave

Magic V...

Cedric's Cave

Wendy's House

Lake

Wiffen's and Perry's Cottage

Echo Men's Castle

Sugar Bread Mines

Turkey Farm

1

The King of the Castle

TITCH AND MITCH WERE RIDING THEIR
magic bicycle home one day after a visit to see their
friend Wendy. They were glad to leave the town
where human people lived, and were looking forward
to a rest on their island, when a large shadow
suddenly covered them. Looking up, they found a
huge bird flying overhead.

"What on earth is that bird?" asked a startled
Titch.

"I believe it's called an albatross, one of the
biggest birds in the world," replied Mitch.

"But why is it flying so close to us?"

There was no chance to call out to the large bird

as it suddenly dropped down to fly underneath them. Then with a quick flap of its long wings, it rose up until the two pixies and the magic bicycle were actually sitting on its back. Another quick wiggle of its wings and the two brothers were tipped off the bicycle.

"Hey, what's going on?" called out Titch in alarm.

Slowly the albatross rose higher and higher and before long they were flying over the island where the two pixies lived.

"That's our home down there," Mitch shouted to the bird. "Put us down please."

"We were going home anyway," said Titch emphatically. "Come on Mitch, we'll fly down to the ground ourselves."

But before they could climb onto the bicycle, the albatross tilted its wings and tipped itself sideways. Titch and Mitch squealed with shock and grabbed handfuls of feathers to stop themselves from falling off. Unfortunately, the magic bicycle slid off the back of the albatross and went tumbling to the ground below.

"Why did you do that?" called out Titch in a very angry tone.

The albatross turned its head slightly and spoke with a very deep voice, "You two are coming with me."

"Why?" Mitch shouted back.

"The King of the Castle wants a pixie."

"What for?" Titch had never heard of the King of the Castle.

"I don't know," rumbled the big bird. "He just said he wanted a pixie and he has paid me very well to get one."

"We demand to be put down. We are not going to this King fellow." Titch was very angry at losing the magic bicycle and being kidnapped by a big bird.

The albatross rumbled again, "Please be quiet, we've got a long way to go."

No matter how much the pixies protested, the albatross ignored them and flew steadily on, leaving their island far behind and heading out to sea.

After what seemed like an age, the bird started to lose height. Peeping over its shoulder, the pixies saw a strange and unfamiliar island looming in the distance. As they got nearer, they could see a large castle right in the middle of the island, with four tall towers stretching high into the sky. When they reached the castle, the albatross floated gently down over the walls and landed in the central courtyard. As the big bird folded its wings, the two brothers tumbled to the ground. The bird looked around.

"Ah, here they come," it rumbled. "I probably won't see you two again, so goodbye." The albatross

took a few steps forward and
jumped up into the air. It
flapped its wings vigorously,
flew over the walls and
disappeared out to sea.

As soon as he was
gone, six large rabbits,
with soldiers sitting
on their backs
and riding them
like horses, came
bounding up. The soldiers wore red tunics and
pointed helmets. They were about the same size as
the pixies with spiky black beards, which made them
look very fierce. They surrounded the two pixies.
Titch and Mitch looked around for an escape route,
but there was nowhere to run.

"You will come with us," said one of the soldiers.

"Where are you taking us?" asked Mitch.

"To meet the king."

"Why?"

But there was no response. Nudging the pixies
roughly, the rabbits and the soldiers escorted them
across the courtyard, up some wide stone steps, and
into a grand hall where the king waited. He was
seated on a large cushion and had a very fat tummy.

On his head there was a golden crown, which covered most of his forehead. Two little eyes peered out over chubby cheeks and, like the guards, he had a black, spiky beard that bobbed up and down when he spoke.

"AT LAST," he said in a very loud voice. "A REAL PIXIE HAS ARRIVED. MY WITCH WILL BE EVER SO PLEASED TO SEE YOU."

"WHAT DO YOU WANT WITH US?" Titch shouted back, angry at being spoken to so rudely.

"SILENCE!" roared the king. "YOU ARE NOT ALLOWED TO SPEAK TO A KING! YOU ARE ONLY A PIXIE. TAKE THEM TO WITCH HAZEL

IMMEDIATELY."

Another set of guards marched them through an archway and up some more steps, which were narrow and winding and led to the top floor of the castle. There, at the start of a long corridor was another guard, standing to attention, outside a strong, wooden door.

"Open the door," demanded the leading guard.

The door creaked as it opened and the two

brothers were pushed inside.

It was gloomy inside the room, but they could make out a hunched figure, dressed in a black robe, sitting in the corner by a window. The witch had a pointed hat with a wide brim, a big nose shaped like a hook, and black eyes that peered at the pixies.

The two brothers shrank into a corner as far from the witch as they could get and clutched each other in fright. The room was cold. The stone walls were damp and slimy. They were locked up in a prison with a witch and there seemed to be no escape.

For a while, they stared in horror at the witch,

and she stared right back at them. Then, to their surprise, the witch's white face crumpled and tears started to roll down her cheeks. Turning away from them, she started to cry softly and muttered, "Oh dear, oh dear, oh dear."

"What's the matter?" asked Mitch in surprise.

"I'm so sorry," she said. "I never thought he would actually find a pixie."

Titch stopped shaking with fright, let go of Mitch and boldly asked, "What on earth are you talking about? Why are we here? Why are you here? What is going on?"

"Please call me Hazel," said the witch, as she stood up and, in a rather bent way, ambled round the room as if wondering what to say next. "Don't be frightened," she said at last in a soft voice. "Not all witches are bad you know. I've always tried to help people. But really, I like to be left alone."

The witch stopped by the window and the two pixies could see that she had a sad, lined face and looked very old.

"Well," she began, "it started about a week ago. I was flying on my broomstick over this island, when I felt very tired, so I landed well away from the castle in a nice, shady spot and settled down for a nap. The next thing I knew, some soldiers in red tunics were

waking me up very rudely. There were a lot of them, and they had grabbed my broomstick so I couldn't escape. I am absolutely lost without my broomstick, it's magic and I need it to make spells and fly wherever I want. Anyway, I was dragged to the castle and made to kneel in front of this horrid, little, fat man with a spiky beard who shouted all the time. He said he was a king and, because I was a witch, he wanted me to do a spell for him or he'd feed me to the sharks. He really frightened me." Hazel stopped talking and cried a little.

"Go on," said Mitch gently. "What happened next?"

"This horrid king person demanded that I create a

spell to make him thin. He said he had been waiting
to catch a witch for years, and now he had one he
was going to be thin once more. I can't do spells like
that." Hazel started to cry again.

"Please don't cry," said Mitch. "But tell us, why
does he want a pixie? We can't do spells either."

"The king didn't believe me, so he locked me up
here and said if I didn't have a spell by the morning,
it was the sharks for me. He's such a horrid
creature!"

"So what did you do?"

"I made up a spell, thinking of some difficult
ingredients, and
hoping he would
never be able to
find them. But
he did." This
time the witch
broke down and
sobbed.

After a while,
she silently
thrust a piece of
paper out from
under her cloak.
It had writing on

it, so Titch took it out of her hand and walked over to the window to read it. He read it out loud for Mitch to hear.

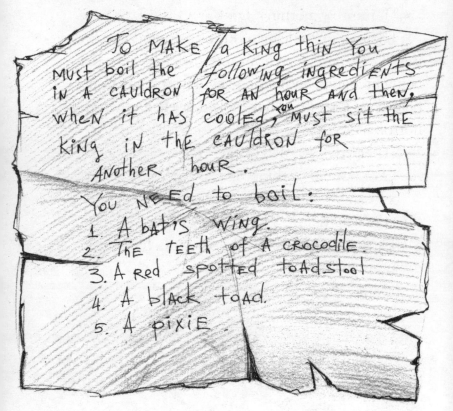

To MAKE a King thin You MusT boil the following ingredients iN A CAuldRON foR AN hour ANd theN, wheN it hAS cooled, you MusT sit thE King iN thE cAuldRoN foR ANotheR hour.

You NEEd to boil:
1. A bAt's WiNg.
2. ThE TEETh of A cRocodile.
3. A Red spoTTEd toAdstool
4. A blAck toAd.
5. A pixiE.

"A PIXIE!" roared Titch and Mitch together. "Are you stark, raving bonkers? A pixie indeed!"

The witch sobbed even louder and muttered, "I'm so sorry, I really am. I just thought that pixies are so very rare that the king would never ever find one and then he would have to let me go."

"When are you supposed to boil this pixie in a cauldron?" asked Titch.

"Tomorrow morning. Look out of the window."

The two pixies leaned out of the window. Down in the courtyard beneath them they saw a bonfire being prepared, with a huge cauldron ready to be placed on top of it. They looked at each other in horror.

"That's it," said Titch. "We'd better get out of here fast! Get your thinking cap on Mitch."

Sitting cross-legged on the floor, the two friends thought very hard. At a loss for any good ideas, Mitch looked up at the ceiling. There, he saw something which surprised him.

"Is that a trap door in the ceiling?" he said, pointing to a little square above them.

"It certainly looks like one," said Titch, leaping to his feet. "Come on Hazel, we need your help."

Witch Hazel stood up and Mitch climbed onto her shoulders. Then, Titch climbed even higher and stood on Mitch's shoulders. It was just high enough for him to reach the trap door. He pushed at the little, square door and it opened to reveal a dark passage. Pulling himself up and through the opening, Titch turned round and dragged Mitch up behind him. As Witch Hazel was too big and heavy for them to pull up as well, they said they would try to come back for her if they could.

"Wait a minute," said Hazel. "You need to find my broomstick. When you do, take it outside and it will fly you up to this window, then we can all escape."

"Great idea," said Mitch. "But where do we look?"

"Everywhere. It's in the castle somewhere. Whilst you look, keep calling out the magic words, 'I Spy Cat's Eye!' and if it hears you, it will come rushing out to find you. When you get outside, sit on the broomstick, hold on very tight and say the magic words, 'Cat's Eye, Fly High!'. Then it'll take you wherever you want to go. It's really the only way we can escape."

"All right," said Titch. "We'll try. Goodbye for now."

The two brothers set out crawling along the passage, which went above all the rooms on the top floor. Each time they passed a trap door, they opened it up and peeped inside. The first room was empty, but they thought it would be too near the guard standing outside the door to Witch Hazel's room, so they crawled along to the last trap door they could find. Opening it up and peeping through, they found the room beneath them was also empty, so they dropped down into it and tiptoed over to the door. Opening it ever so slightly, they peeped out and into a long corridor. Ahead of them, they saw the guard

outside Hazel's door.

"He's looking the other way," whispered Mitch. "Let's run to the staircase."

"OK," Titch whispered back. "Go!"

They scampered out of the room and across to a staircase that led to the floors beneath them.

"What now?" asked Mitch.

"I think we should go to the ground floor and work our way up. We go into every room. If the coast is clear we call out, 'I Spy Cat's Eye'. Then, if the broomstick rushes out to us, we grab it and flee outside to the courtyard."

Carefully, the pixies crept down the stairs to the ground floor. On the way, they stopped for a moment to look out of a window. Down in the courtyard, they saw many soldiers marching to and fro. Huge crowds of people were milling about watching them, obviously waiting for something to happen.

"There's something going on out there," said Titch.

"Good," said Mitch. "It means there'll be fewer people in the castle. Let's hurry while we can."

On the ground floor, they opened the first door they came to and peeped inside. It was a kitchen and little people in white coats were busy rushing round and preparing food. Some of them turned to look at the pixies, but nobody seemed to be interested in them at all.

"I Spy Cat's Eye!" called out Titch, anxiously. He got some strange looks from the cooks, but there was no response from the broomstick. Closing the door, they moved on to the next room. It was empty.

"I Spy Cat's Eye!" Mitch called out loudly. But there was no response.

When they got to the very last room along the corridor, they opened the door and called out again, "I Spy Cat's Eye!"

Unfortunately, they had not noticed a soldier

leaning out of the window and watching the people outside. When they called out the words, two things happened. First, there was a clattering and a knocking inside a cupboard by the side of them and, second, the soldier turned round and spotted them. He gave out a roar and rushed at them.

Quick as a flash, Titch opened the cupboard door and immediately the broomstick fell out. They had no time to pick it up, because the guard was almost upon them, so they turned and fled. The guard chased them down the corridor and the pixies raced in front of him, heading for the main door.

Meanwhile, the broomstick picked itself up and flew out of the room, looking for the person who had called out 'I Spy Cat's Eye!'. It flew past the guard and caught up with the pixies just as they got to the main door. Luckily, the door was open, so Titch raced out, followed by Mitch and the soldier, who roared to all the people outside, "Stop the pixies! Catch them before they escape!"

Titch and Mitch fled past the platform where the king sat. He was waving his hands and roaring like everyone else. Finally, Titch and Mitch had nowhere to go, so they stopped and looked around. The broomstick also stopped and hovered right alongside them.

"Quick," said Mitch. "Get on the broomstick!"

Titch sat on the long broomstick and wrapped his legs round it. The soldiers were surrounding him, and reaching out to grab him, when he called out loudly, "Cat's Eye, Fly High!"

Mitch didn't have enough time to get his seat, so he just hung on with both hands. Immediately, the broomstick flew out of the reach of all the people chasing them. Higher and higher they went, until they reached the top of the castle tower. Titch slipped over sideways, but managed to hang on with both his hands. The broomstick started to fly around

in circles with the two pixies dangling beneath it, when a thin voice floated over to them, "Over here, Kitten. Come to mummy."

The broomstick instantly changed direction and soared towards Witch Hazel, who was leaning out of the window of her cell, calling to them. "This way, come to me," she cried.

The people and the soldiers below them watched and roared with rage as the broomstick and the pixies flew towards the witch's room. Suddenly, they all turned round and raced back into the castle, determined to get to the witch's room first and stop her escaping. But it was too late; the broomstick had reached the room on the top floor.

"Hold on to me," ordered Hazel, as she climbed on to the broomstick. The pixies picked themselves off the floor where they had collapsed and climbed up behind Hazel. Titch clutched the witch round the waist and Mitch clutched Titch very tightly round his

waist. Just then, the door burst open and the guards rushed in, followed by the angry mob, but could only watch as Hazel, the broomstick and the two pixies flew out of the window and headed straight out to sea, away from the King of the Castle and his island.

It was a long, cold journey, but the broomstick went a lot faster than the albatross had, and when their own little island came into view, they were very relieved to be getting home. Directing Hazel to their little cottage, they zoomed down to land in the garden.

"It's nice to be home," said Mitch. "But I'm so

sorry we lost the magic bicycle. It was quite horrid of that bird to tip it off its back."

"Maybe it's somewhere on the island," replied Titch. "We were flying over it at the time, if I remember."

The three of them went inside the house to make a cup of tea and rest their aching bodies. However, as soon as they settled down on the sofa, there was a knock on the door.

"Hello," said old Mr Beaver, with a smile on his whiskery face. "Have you lost a bicycle?" Behind him, their magic bicycle sat on the ground as if it had never left the garden.

Titch and Mitch were amazed. "Where did you find it?" they asked with great relief.

"It landed in our lake with an enormous splash

and sank right to the bottom. The little ones fished it out and said it belonged to you two. We were very worried about you. We thought you might have fallen in the lake as well. I am so relieved to find you both safe. You must tell me what happened."

"We will, one day, but thank you so much for rescuing our bicycle."

2

The Cuckoo Clock

AS ALL THEIR FRIENDS KNEW, TITCH AND
Mitch were very fond of cakes and pastries, but their
favourite of all was strawberry tart. Their friend
Wendy always had a slice with a glass of milk when
she came home from school. When the pixies went
to visit, they made sure to arrive just before she came
home in the afternoon so that she would share her
tart and milk with them. It was something they did
very often these days, as Wendy had some of the best
strawberry tart they had ever tasted.

One day, they flew their magic bicycle to the town
where Wendy lived and landed on the roof of her
house. After tying the bicycle to the television aerial

next to the chimney pot, the pixies slid down the chimney. They squealed and laughed all the way down and finally tumbled into Wendy's playroom and sat on the carpet dusting themselves off. As they were a little bit early, they went over to Wendy's doll's house and opened the door, intending to settle themselves inside and give their friend a surprise. But when they looked inside, they stopped in astonishment; the furniture was gone.

"Where's the sofa?" asked Titch as he looked around, "and the big armchair?"

Before Mitch could reply, the door to the playroom opened and they heard a man's voice call out, "I'll leave the new doll's house in Wendy's

39

playroom, my dear. It will be a nice birthday surprise
for her."

The two brothers peeped out of the window and
saw a brand new and very splendid doll's house
placed on the carpet next to them. Then they heard
Wendy's mother reply, "And chuck the old one out;
the bin men are coming."

The man picked up the old doll's house and the
two pixies held on to each other.

"Oh no," cried Titch, "where are we going?"

"You heard Wendy's mum," replied Mitch. "We're being thrown out."

The doll's house was stuffed in the bin outside the house and Titch and Mitch were left alone and upside down in the dark.

As they were trying to clamber out, they heard the loud rumbling of the refuse collection lorry coming along the road. Before they knew it, the bin was lifted in the air, and with a clatter and a bang, was dumped inside the lorry.

A very uncomfortable journey followed. Every few minutes another bin was tipped on top of them until

the lorry was full.

"Where will we end up?" wailed Mitch.

"We must be going to the dump, wherever that is," replied his brother.

Eventually, after what seemed an eternity, the lorry stopped. With a great roar, all the rubbish was tipped out. Titch and Mitch were thrown head over heels and bounced around inside the doll's house, until finally everything went very quiet.

Mitch gingerly picked himself up and peeped out

of the window. All he could see were old boxes, pieces of paper, bricks and all manner of things that human people throw out.

"How are we going to get home?" he cried.

"At least we're still alive with no bones broken, and our doll's house is on top of the dump, not squashed under all the rubbish," replied Titch, looking on the bright side.

The two brothers squeezed themselves out of the broken doll's house and sat on the roof. They were

completely lost and had no idea how to find Wendy's house or their magic bicycle.

"I don't like being lost," Mitch said, in a very unhappy voice.

"Neither do I," agreed Titch, in an equally unhappy voice.

They sat with their heads cupped in their hands for ages, with no idea where to go.

Suddenly, Mitch sat up and looked around. "I just heard a strange noise," he said.

"What sort of a noise?"

"It was a sort of a bird noise. It sounded like a cuckoo."

"Well, it is April you know. Cuckoos are always calling out in April."

"But this noise is coming from underneath us."

"Cuckoos live in trees," said Titch, very irritated at being disturbed when he was trying hard to think. "They don't live under piles of rubbish."

"Yes, there it goes again." Mitch stood up and started to clamber towards the noise.

Reluctantly, Titch followed him and soon he also heard the sound of a cuckoo calling. Finally, they stood quite still and listened carefully.

"Cuckoo, cuckoo, cuckoo," they heard, clearly.

"It's coming from under our feet," exclaimed

Mitch in surprise.

Immediately the two brothers started digging and scrabbling at the piles of rubbish. They heaved empty tins, crushed cartons and various other bits of rubbish out of the way until finally the front of an old clock was revealed. As they paused to get their breath back, they heard the call again, only this time it was much louder, "CUCKOO, CUCKOO."

"My goodness!" exclaimed Titch. "It's coming from the clock."

Above the numbers around the face of the clock there was a little door with a heart-shaped hole in it and a small handle. They grabbed this, pulled hard, and opened the door. A brown cuckoo with black eyes, a yellow beak, and very ruffled feathers poked its head out and said, "Cuckoo. Thank you for opening the door. I've been locked inside for ages."

Tears began to roll down the bird's cheeks as she started to cry. "It was so dark and smelly and horrid down there." The poor bird choked, sobbed and, after climbing out of the clock, collapsed in a heap beside Titch and Mitch. "Thank you so much for letting me out," they heard the poor bird mutter.

Titch and Mitch felt very sorry for the cuckoo and they searched around to find her some food and water. Very quickly they discovered a tin can full of rainwater and a crust of dry bread in a brown paper bag. The cuckoo was very grateful and pecked and drank until she felt much better.

"I'm Cleo," she said. "Who are you? I've never seen human people as small as you two." She tilted her head and looked quizzically at the curious pair.

"We are pixies. My name is Titch and my brother here is called Mitch."

"I'm so very pleased to meet you." Cleo flapped her wings and ruffled her feathers so that she quivered all over.

"Why were you in that clock?" asked Titch, full of curiosity.

"Because I am a very silly and a very greedy bird!" said Cleo sadly and, brushing a clump of dust off her wing, she continued, "I was hunting around the edge of the rubbish dump looking for scraps to eat, when I came across a few pieces of malt bread. Well, I just can't resist malt bread, especially as these pieces were fresh, with butter all over them. Honestly, you'd be amazed at the things people throw away. Anyway, I gobbled them up, then I found a few more pieces, and then a few more, until, finally, I came across an old clock with its door open. Inside was more malt bread and some

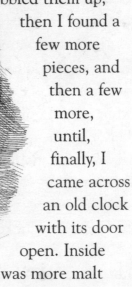

currants! Naturally, I climbed into the clock and finished off all the bread and currants and then, as I turned to go, the door was slammed shut. I was locked inside the clock."

"Oh dear," cried Mitch. "What made the door close?"

"A very naughty boy! I stuck my head out of the hole and saw a boy in school uniform standing there, jumping up and down with delight. 'I've caught a cuckoo!' he kept shouting. 'Now, I've got a real cuckoo clock!'"

"Why did he want to have a cuckoo in a clock?" asked Mitch in surprise.

"The boy came right up to the clock and said to me – 'Cuckoo, you must stick your head out of the clock every hour and call 'CUCKOO, CUCKOO, CUCKOO'.' Then he stuck his face close to the

clock and tried to peep inside. So I stuck my head
out of the hole and pecked him as hard as I could,
right on his nose."

"Well done," said Titch. "That served him right!
It was very naughty to lock you up. Fancy trying to
turn you into a cuckoo clock!"

"The boy jumped in the air with surprise when I
pecked him. Then he said he was going to take me

home in the clock and I'd be locked up for ever! And every hour I'd have to stick my head out of the window and call out 'cuckoo', so people would know what time it was. Then he picked up the clock and tried to stuff it in his bag, but it wouldn't fit, so he left it by the side of the rubbish tip and told me he'd be back the next morning to collect me."

"How awful for you!" said Titch, full of sympathy for poor Cleo.

"But he never came back. I never saw the horrid little boy again. I spent the whole night in the clock and I kept calling out, but the only thing that found me was a large rat with yellow, gleaming eyes. He wanted to get me out and eat me! Luckily, he

51

couldn't open the door. After that, I stopped calling out and waited until morning. But then, as soon as it was daylight, a great big, yellow digger came along, scooped up the clock with a load of other rubbish, and dumped it all into the middle of the tip. Everything went dark until you two came along and got me out. I dread to think what might have happened."

"It's lucky for you we came along," said Mitch.

"Look, over there," Cleo, pointed to a big, mechanical digger. "That's the beast. Keep an eye on it. Once it starts to move, nobody's safe!"

The two pixies stared at the digger on the edge of the rubbish dump. Inside they could see a driver, with his feet up on the steering wheel, eating a huge burger out of a plastic box.

"He's having a break," observed Mitch. "We should be safe for a while."

"So, what are you two doing on a rubbish tip?" asked Cleo. "You don't look like you live here."

"It's a long story," said Titch, and proceeded to tell Cleo about how they were inside the doll's house when it was thrown onto the tip.

"Maybe I can help you?" she offered, keen to repay the favour.

"If you can think of a way to get us back to Wendy's house, we would be very grateful," said Mitch, hopefully.

"We don't want to spend a night here among all the rubbish, especially if there are hungry rats around," added Titch, shivering at the very thought.

"Let me see if I can fly over the town and see where exactly this house is. How will I recognise it?"

"It's a detached house with a big tree in the garden, a red roof and a bicycle tied to a television aerial, next to the chimney pot," said Titch. "You can't miss it."

"Leave it to me," said Cleo, and she took to the

sky with a delighted flutter, soaring high into the air and very relieved to have escaped from inside the clock. Titch and Mitch decided to return to the doll's house and watch for Cleo the cuckoo through the windows. All the talk of large, fierce rats had unnerved them both.

The daylight was starting to dim when Cleo returned and landed right next to the doll's house. "It was easy to find," she said, very proudly. "It's the only house in the whole town with a bicycle on the roof."

"How far away is it?" asked Titch.

"A long way. You could never walk there, too many people, cars and busy roads. And it will be dark soon." Cleo lifted her head and looked anxiously to the sky.

"What are we going to do?" wailed Mitch.

"Perhaps we could barricade ourselves into the doll's

house and wait for morning?"

"I've got an idea," said Cleo. "I'm too small to carry either of you, but I'm sure my mother could carry you both together."

Titch and Mitch looked very doubtful. "Your mother would have to be a lot bigger than you are," said Mitch.

"My mother is a barn owl," said Cleo, "and she's huge!"

"How can your mother be a barn owl?" Titch was amazed. "You're a cuckoo."

"Well, it's like this," Cleo settled down as if the story could take a long time. "Cuckoos never build nests," she said, looking at them curiously. "I thought everybody knew that."

The two pixies shook their heads.

"Cuckoos always lay their eggs in the nests of other birds," continued Cleo. "My real mother was a cuckoo, of course, and she laid her egg in the nest of a barn owl. It was a very big and very comfortable nest and when I hatched out my new mother owl wasn't deceived at all, but thought I was cute and adopted me. She looked after me until I was quite big. I often go back home to see her, so I'm sure she will help me if I ask her."

"Great," said Titch, who cheered up as he realised

they might soon be able to leave the rubbish tip.

"Unfortunately, there is a bit of a problem. As you know, owls sleep during the day and don't wake up until it's dark. My Mother Owl gets very bad tempered if I wake her too early, and she might sulk for days, so I have to be very careful."

"Perhaps if you wake her with a titbit she'd be pleased with you. What is her favourite food?" asked Titch.

Cleo looked

thoughtful. "First of all she likes mice, then she likes toads, rats and, of course, big spiders are very tasty."

"Yuck!" said Titch in disgust. "There is no way we can catch any of those. In fact it's more likely that a rat would catch us first."

"I hate rats!" added Mitch.

"I once saw her eat some chocolate and she said it was delicious," said Cleo. "She also likes cakes and ice cream."

Suddenly, the yellow digger roared into life as the driver started his engine and the huge machine jerked and rolled slowly across the tip towards them.

"I think we'd better run," cried Mitch.

"Which way?" replied Titch.

"Away from the digger, of course."

They scrambled over rubbish as fast as they could and then turned to see if the digger was still following them. It was and, worse still, it had disturbed a gathering of rats who also ran away from the digger and were heading straight for them.

"Oh no!" cried Mitch and he turned and started to run even faster. Titch followed, but the rats were faster and soon caught up with them. Mitch wailed, thinking they were all about to be nibbled to pieces, but as the rats were trying to escape from the digger as well, they simply ran past the pixies and headed towards a big, black hole in the ground. One large rat looked at Titch as he went by and, with a wide grin, called out, "Run, little one! If the digger doesn't get you, we will!"

The rats raced on and left them alone, but before the digger reached them, it stopped. The driver turned off the engine, stepped down from his cab and walked away towards a small wooden hut that stood

at the edge of the dump.

Immediately, they stopped to get their breath back and Cleo swooped down to join them. "I wonder if that driver has left any tasty titbits in his cab?" Cleo said, thoughtfully. "I'll just fly over and take a peek."

A few moments later Cleo returned. "There's a bar of chocolate on the seat," she squeaked with excitement. "I peeped inside and saw it lying there. The window's wide open. Come on, pixies, let's get

the chocolate!"

While Cleo fluttered around in the sky, Titch and
Mitch helped each other to climb onto the digger's
step, then up onto the front wheel. With a jump,
Titch grabbed the edge of the window and leapt
down onto the drivers seat. Quickly, he grabbed the
bar of chocolate and passed it out to Mitch, who
held it high in the air. Cleo swooped down, snatched
the chocolate right out of his hand, and in no time at
all, the cuckoo had disappeared into the distance.
The two pixies then made their way back to the
doll's house.

While they waited for Cleo and her mother to

return, they looked for a bag which the owl could easily carry in her beak, and was also strong enough to hold two pixies. At the same time, they noticed how dark it was getting and both kept a sharp watch for the rats, in case they came back to get them.

It was dusk when, with a cry of 'cuckoo, cuckoo', Cleo returned. A few moments later, her mother owl

landed beside the doll's house. She was a very big owl with large, dark brown eyes and a curved beak.

"Chocolate indeed," said the owl. "What a treat! I have saved most of it for my tea later. I am pleased to meet you both. Please call me Mother Owl, everybody does."

"We don't want to spend the night here," said Mitch, anxiously. "Can you help us get to Wendy's house?"

"Of course," said Mother Owl, "but what can I carry you in?"

Mitch held up the bag they had found. It was a ripped, cloth bag from a supermarket. "Will this do?" he asked.

"Just the job," said mother owl. "Jump in and we'll be off. Cleo can show me the way. Is it light enough for you to see your way?" she asked Cleo.

"Yes, but be quick and follow me."

With Cleo leading and mother owl flying just behind her, they set off. Titch and Mitch were scrunched up in the bag, but they managed to peep out and see the town passing by beneath them. When they saw their magic bicycle on the roof, they called out to Mother Owl, "There! Right below us! That's Wendy's house. Look, Cleo is already perched on the edge of the chimney pot. Put us down Mother Owl."

Unfortunately, Mother Owl forgot she was carrying a bag in her beak and replied. "I see it," she called out. "Ohhhh no!"

It was too late. The bag slipped out of her beak as soon as she opened it. It dropped down, gathering

speed, whizzed passed Cleo, and fell straight down the chimney.

"Goodbye. I'll come and visit," they heard Cleo call as they bumped and banged their way down the chimney.

Once again, they shot out onto the floor of Wendy's playroom and clambered out of the bag. The room was dark but Mitch used the hawk's feather to provide light. There, right in front of them, was the new doll's house, bigger and better by far than the last one.

"Let's explore inside," said Mitch.

The two pixies opened the door of the doll's

house and went in.

"This is a beautiful little house," said Mitch in delight. "Those new beds look very comfortable, and I don't think we can fly the magic bicycle home in the dark. Shall we spend the night here?"

"Yes," said Titch, "and when the family have gone to bed, we can go into the kitchen and look for some of those cakes that Wendy's mother makes!"

3

The Red Crabs

"MONSTERS! MONSTERS!" CRIED MOLLY
rabbit as she raced into Titch and Mitch's garden.
The two pixies had just finished their lunch and were
looking forward to an afternoon nap, when Molly
arrived quite out of breath and extremely distraught.

"What are you talking about, Molly?" asked
Mitch.

"On the beach, there are millions of great, red
monsters coming out of the sea! They're all over the
beach with more and more coming ashore all the
time. I must warn mummy and daddy, we have to
flee!" Molly turned round, ran out of the garden and
set off towards the woods, crying out as loudly as she

could, "Flee everybody! The monsters are coming!"

On the island where Titch and Mitch lived, there was just one tiny beach, reached by a small path that wound its way down the cliffs. The two pixies often spent sunny days there and always had the beach to themselves.

"We'd better go and have a look and see what that silly rabbit is talking about," said Mitch. "It's probably just a pile of seaweed or something that has been washed up by the tide." But even as he spoke, he felt a bit uneasy, as Molly had obviously been most upset by what she had seen.

It was only a short journey along the meadow and past the woods to the top of the cliffs, so Titch and Mitch got there quickly and took the path to the beach. It was a very steep and winding path, and

they were half way down when Titch pulled up
suddenly and held out his arm to stop Mitch.

"I can hear something. What is it?" he asked, in a
puzzled voice.

"It's a sort of clicking noise," said Mitch,
thoughtfully.

The two brothers leaned over the rocks that edged the path and gazed down at the scene below.

"Look at all those crabs!" exclaimed Titch in surprise. "They're everywhere. I can't see any sand. There are massive red crabs all over the beach! Where on earth did they come from?"

Mitch was quite taken aback. "I've never seen crabs that big before. And look! There are hundreds more crawling out of the sea."

Sure enough, the waves lapping onto the beach were bubbling and frothing with a huge number of crabs, all struggling to get to the shore and join their friends. The clicking noise came from all those crabs snapping their pincers together repeatedly.

Just at that moment, a singularly large red crab walked round the corner of the path and stopped right in front of them. It was the same height as the pixies, but very much wider. In fact, it looked like a great, red dinner plate with eight legs. However, what frightened the pixies most were the two, huge pincer claws it held high in the air.

The two brothers turned to flee, but the crab whistled after them and said, "Hello there. Please don't run away. I hope you don't mind us using your beach." The crab had a soft voice and seemed quite friendly.

The pixies had run a short way back up the path, but curiosity made them stop and, looking apprehensively at the monster crab, Titch said, "Who are you? What are you doing on the beach? How long are you staying?"

The crab laughed. "One question at a time please. First of all, we are giant red crabs from the far north, and every ten years we come to a secluded beach to crown our new queen. If you look down at the shore, by that rock in the middle of the sand, you will see

her." The red crab sounded very proud and said, "Isn't she beautiful!"

Titch and Mitch looked down at the seething mass of crabs and, to be honest, they all looked very much the same.

"Er... Which one is the queen?" asked Titch, staring hard at the crabs surrounding the small rock.

"She's not as big as the guards around her, and she's got a streak of purple on her shell, just behind her eyes. You can't miss her, she's gorgeous!" The red crab looked hard at Titch and frowned.

Hastily, Titch said, "Oh yes, of course. I see her now."

This pleased the big red crab and he returned to staring at the beach below them. Titch looked at Mitch and shrugged his shoulders. He really had no idea which was the new queen of the crabs.

The crab sighed with pleasure. "Soon we'll be placing the crown on her head and then we'll all cheer and click as loudly as we can. You can watch if you like, but promise not to come down the path any further. I'm a guard sent to make sure that nobody interrupts the crowning ceremony."

"Oh, we'll certainly promise not to go down to the beach. There's no room anyway, and with all that clicking going on, I think we will stay here and watch the ceremony," Mitch was quite emphatic.

"Look now," said the crab. "There's the crown." The guard crab danced up and down on all his legs, waved his huge pincer claws wildly, and sounded very excited.

Titch and Mitch could certainly see the crown

and had to agree that it was quite magnificent. Several crabs were pushing and helping the new queen to climb onto the rock, which was obviously going to be her throne, while two of the guard crabs held the crown high in the air as they brought it forward.

The crown sparkled in the sunshine and Titch and Mitch could see it was made from many precious stones and pearls. The light bounced off the coloured stones so that it gleamed and sparkled.

"I'd love to go and cheer," said the excited crab,

"but I'm supposed to stay here and watch this path."
He looked at the two friends doubtfully. "I say you
two, you look decent sorts. Would you mind guarding
this path for me? I'd really love to go and click with
my friends."

"Oh yes, of course we will," said Mitch. "We don't
mind watching from here, and I can assure you there
won't be anybody coming down this path today."

"Excellent!" shouted the red crab, and
immediately scuttled off round the corner and back
down the path to the beach.

Moments later the noise rose to a crescendo of
clicking and scratching as the queen, now settled on
the rock, awaited the arrival of the crown, which was
being passed high in the air towards her.

It was then that a black and white bird came
swooping down towards the beach with one thing on
its mind, the crown. Magpies cannot resist shiny,
sparkling things, and the crown had caught the eye
of this particular magpie. With a tilt of its head and a
snatch of its beak, the bird picked the crown right
out of the claws of the crabs and flew up into the air.

Unfortunately, it flew right towards Titch and
Mitch, who leaped to their feet, shouting and waving
at the magpie to try and stop it. The bird flew right
over them, coming so close that Titch jumped as

high as he could to try to grab the crown, but he couldn't quite reach and they watched helplessly as the bird soared up to the top of the cliff and disappeared.

For a moment, there was a stunned silence on the beach. Then, the voice of the guard they had met earlier rang out loud and clear, "Those two pixies made the bird steal our crown! AFTER THEM!"

In one movement, all the crabs on the beach swivelled towards the path and saw the two pixies

standing there. A great roar went up and the loud
clicking started again, only this time there was a lot
of angry hissing as well, and the crabs all raced
towards the cliff.

Titch and Mitch watched, amazed at the speed
the crabs could move. When they realized that
thousands of crabs were heading towards them intent
on vengeance, the two pixies turned and fled. By the
time they reached the top of the cliff, they were out
of breath and quite exhausted.

"To the woods," cried Titch, when they had
crossed the meadow. "We'll never make it home.
Those crabs are moving too fast."

Sure enough, as they looked behind them, they
saw the crabs had already reached the meadow and
were spreading out across the grass in hot pursuit.

With the crabs gaining on them rapidly, Titch and
Mitch reached the wood and climbed up the first tree

they came to. Luckily, it was a big tree so the pixies climbed as high as they could before looking down. Beneath them, stretched out across the meadow, was a great red tide of crabs, hissing, scratching and clicking with anger.

As they watched in horror, a yellow bird flew into the tree and landed on the branch they were clinging to. Startled, Titch and Mitch looked round.

"Budgie," they cried out together. "We are so glad to see you."

"We need some help," said Mitch, relieved to see their seagull friend.

"We need a lot of help," added Titch.

"Please tell me," said Budgie, "why are those crabs chasing you and where did they come from?"

Titch gave a brief explanation. "They came out of the sea, thousands of them, to crown their new queen. But a wretched magpie swooped down and

77

snatched the crown in its beak and made off with it."

"But why do they blame you two?" asked Budgie, curiously.

"Well, we were watching from that little path that leads down to the beach. Unfortunately, the magpie flew right over our heads. The crabs thought the bird had stolen the crown and given it to us! When really, we were just trying to stop the magpie from flying

away with it!" Titch gasped, hanging on to the branch with both hands.

"It's a good job crabs can't climb trees," observed Budgie. "How can I help?"

"You have to get the crown back for us." Mitch had to shout to make himself heard above the noise of angry crabs below.

"How do I do that?"

"Find the magpie's nest and steal the crown back," Titch said, thinking this to be a good idea.

But Budgie shook her head. "I can't do that! There are hundreds of birds on the island, and they

all have nests. It would take me weeks to check them all."

Mitch began to wail. "What are we going to do? I can't sit on this branch for ever. If I fall off, those monstrous red crabs will gobble me up."

"Please be quiet Mitch, I've got another idea," said Titch, hitting on a new plan of action. "Listen carefully Budgie. Fly to our house by the stream and inside you will find a small mirror on the table. Drop it on to the floor and break it into tiny pieces, then put the broken glass into a bowl and then bring it back to us."

"Why do you want me to break your mirror?" Budgie asked with surprise.

"Just do it and when you get back here I'll explain."

"All right, all right, I'm off." The yellow seagull flapped into the air and flew straight towards the pixies' house.

In a few minutes, she was back and Titch took the bowl from her beak. "Now then," said Titch, "this is the plan. You fly to the next tree and watch us on this branch. When you see the magpie fly in to steal all these shiny pieces of glass, you follow the thief and find out where it lives. Then, when the magpie leaves its nest, you fly in and grab the crown."

Titch edged his way along the branch until he came to the very tip. There he wedged the bowl in between two small twigs. "Now then Mitch, you climb to the branch above and shine the hawk's feather into the pieces of glass. That will make them sparkle so that the magpie will see them and want to

have them for its nest."

Mitch took the Hawk's feather from his hat. He treasured the feather because Misty, the fairy, had made it magic and it would shine brightly whenever he wanted it to.

"All right Titch, I won't be a minute." Mitch felt a lot more cheerful, now they had a plan. He scrambled up to a higher branch, shone his feather down on the bowl, then hid behind some leaves so he wouldn't scare the magpie when it came.

It seemed ages before anything happened. All the time the crabs below were hissing, clicking and making an awful noise. Just when Mitch thought he couldn't hold his arm out straight any longer, they heard a swishing noise above them. A great black and white bird landed on the branch next to the sparkling bowl. Quick as a flash, the magpie grabbed a beak full of broken glass, flapped its way out of the tree and up into the air.

The two pixies watched anxiously as the magpie flew over the trees. Then, just before it disappeared from view, they saw a yellow bird rise up from a nearby tree and set off in pursuit.

Titch tried to shout down to the crabs and explain what had happened, but they were making so much noise, they couldn't hear a word he said. He

gave up and returned to the branch where he settled himself down next to Mitch to wait for the return of their seagull friend.

"Look," said Mitch, a short while later, "here comes the magpie again!"

Once more, the large black and white bird swooped into the tree. With great speed, it grabbed some more pieces of glass and took off again, heading back the way it had come.

"Hurrah," cried Titch. "That means it's left its nest unguarded, and if Budgie knows where it is, then she must have found the crown."

Sure enough, they saw Budgie flying towards them as fast as she could with something large and sparkling in her beak.

"She's got it!" shouted Mitch with relief. "Hurrah for Budgie!"

However, as they watched the magpie going back to its nest, it passed the yellow seagull coming in the

other direction. The magpie gave a squawk when it saw Budgie with the crown in her beak, and dropped the pieces of glass. Wheeling round, it started chasing after the seagull. The magpie screeched louder and louder as it chased after Budgie, furious that the yellow bird now had the crown. The black and white thief wanted it back.

Budgie was so frightened, she crashed into the tree at high speed and landed on the branch next to Titch. He promptly grabbed the crown and called out to Mitch, "Quick Mitch, use the Hawk's feather!"

Mitch knew what to do. He looked up and the

magpie was almost upon them. It had its claws outstretched and its big beak open, ready for a savage peck. As the magpie rushed into the tree and brushed the leaves aside, Budgie gave a frightened shriek and jumped down onto the branch below. At the same time, Mitch waved the Hawk's feather. Out shot the sparkling light and covered the magpie. The result was startling. The magpie leaped up into the air, banged its head on the branch above, toppled over and fell right out of the tree.

Tumbling to the ground, it landed smack in the middle of the seething mass of angry crabs. It bounced on the broad back of one of the biggest crabs and was just able to struggle to its feet. With a terrified squawk, it flapped its wings desperately in order to get away. It just managed to get airborne in time, losing only a few soft feathers from under its tail. Flying out of the reach of the crabs and having forgotten all about stealing the crown, it flew off and never came back.

Slowly, the hissing and clicking died down. The big crab, who had been bounced on by the fleeing bird, stood up and dusted himself off.

"Sorry, you two," he said, looking up into the tree, and immediately Titch & Mitch recognised the guard. "We didn't realise the magpie had kept the crown. We thought you had stolen it."

The crabs all stood back, allowing Titch and Mitch to climb down out of the tree and hand over the magnificent crown. As they did so, the crabs all started clicking once more, only now they were cheering. Picking up Titch and Mitch gently in his claws, the guard crab placed them on his broad back

and called out, "Three cheers for Titch and Mitch! They got the crown back for our queen, so they can be guests of honour at her coronation and join in our feast. Hurrah! Hurrah! Hurrah!"

The great hoard of red crabs returned to the beach with the two pixies, who were privileged to watch the crowning ceremony and the festivities from a place of honour next to the new queen.

4

The Echo Men

THERE IS A LITTLE STONE COTTAGE IN A clearing in a wood, which is the home of Wiffen, the intelligent turkey, and his friend Perry, an Old English sheepdog.

One day, Titch and Mitch arrived on their magic bicycle, landed in the garden of their two friends, and found Wiffen in quite an agitated state.

"It's a mystery, a total mystery and I don't like a mystery. I am the most intelligent turkey in the whole world but I cannot understand what's going on. It's baffling." Wiffen fluffed up his feathers in agitation, gave an irritated squawk and shuffled round the garden shaking his red wattle furiously.

Perry greeted the two pixies. "I'm so very glad to see you. We have a problem and Wiffen cannot find an answer. As you can see, he's not a happy turkey."

"Perhaps we can help," said Mitch, and, spotting Wiffen glaring at him, added, "Of course, we aren't as clever as Wiffen, but we might be able to help in some small way."

Wiffen stopped shuffling about and said, thoughtfully, "You may indeed be able to help. How long can you stay for?"

"All day and all night if necessary," answered Titch.

Wiffen settled himself down. "This is the problem," he said. "There is a quarry nearby which we call Echo Quarry."

"Why is it called Echo Quarry?" interrupted Mitch.

Wiffen glared at him for a very long moment before replying. "It is called Echo Quarry because, if

you stand in the middle of it and call out your name, or some such thing, then the sound bounces off all four sides of the quarry and you hear your name repeated back at you four times."

"Why four times?" asked Mitch, puzzled.

"Because there are four walls, silly!" sniffed Wiffen.

"However," he continued, "that's not what is worrying us. The problem is that someone, or something, is building a castle in the quarry. We go there every day and each day it gets a little bit bigger. But, and this is the strange thing, we have never caught even the slightest glimpse of whoever is building it. It's driving me mad. Sometimes we sneak up very quietly, and peep over the side of the quarry, but there's nobody working there. We once stayed there all day, hidden behind a rock, but nothing moved, not a thing! But if we leave and go back, there are always some more stones added on to the structure. There is only the roof to go on now, so it's nearly finished."

Perry supported his friend, "We've chatted with Old Bill the badger who lives along the path leading to the quarry, and he says that he's never seen anybody go down to the quarry either. Yet every time we go, there are more stones piled on top of each

other. It is indeed a mystery."

He raised his bushy eyebrows and looked at Wiffen.

"What we need," said the turkey, "is for somebody to stay all day and all night in the castle. Then, whoever sneaks in to build it, and it must be somebody very strong indeed, will be seen by whoever is hiding in the castle."

"Oh, I see," said Mitch. "You want Titch and I to spend all day and all night sitting on stones in the middle of a half-built castle, only to find some hideous monster is building it!"

"No, no, no!" said Wiffen. "Nothing of the sort. Perry and I will spend all day in the castle. You two will take over in the evening."

"And spend all night there!"

Titch thought he had a better idea, "I think we should all go together. As it's the afternoon already, we can take a picnic for this evening, and blankets, then we can all spend the night in the quarry. It'll be quite an adventure!"

He saw Wiffen looking doubtful and added, "We really need somebody very intelligent, and Perry can always bark and frighten monsters away if necessary. Besides, four is more company than two."

"I suppose so," conceded Wiffen.

Everyone agreed this was
the best idea, so they
started to pack up
food and blankets
and set off a short
while later.

Old Bill the
Badger popped
his head out of
his burrow as
they neared the
quarry. "Hello
Wiffen," he said.
"I've been watching out
to see if anyone has gone down into the quarry, but
nothing has passed this way all day. Maybe it's a
ghost building the castle."

"I don't like the idea of meeting a ghost."
muttered Mitch. "Perhaps we should go home and
forget all about it."

"Absolutely not!" cried Wiffen. "Ghosts can't lift
great lumps of rock. And anyway, I don't believe in
ghosts. Thank you for your help, Mr Badger, but we'll
be on our way. We are going to spend the night in
the castle and then we'll find out who is building
down there."

The four friends descended a winding path, and finally came out in the middle of a large semi-circle of scarred rock. Standing in the centre, and towering above them, was the stone castle. Great blocks of stone laid neatly on top of each other made up the walls, and there was a turret at each corner. "Most of the roof is on," called out Wiffen in

a fury. "Who did that?" He looked around, but there was nobody in the quarry and nowhere for anybody to hide. Sure enough, when the two pixies walked round the castle and looked up, there where giant slabs of rock laid end to end that stretched from one wall to the next.

"I wonder who is going to live here when it's finished?" asked Mitch. "If we wait until they move in, we can come and visit."

"Maybe it is a ghost, and they only come out at night," said Titch.

"In which case, we'll see them tonight and that will be an end to the mystery," responded Wiffen, still very grumpy.

The four friends walked around the outside of the castle again, admiring the neat way the builders had placed the stones together so smoothly. Titch suddenly said, "Why haven't we heard an echo yet."

"You have to shout out very loud," said Perry.

Wiffen said to Titch, "Go on! Shout something and see what happens."

Titch took a deep breath and roared out, "HELLO." The noise echoed round the four walls of the quarry. "HELLO," bounced back off the first wall, and then immediately they heard "HELLO" again, as the sound bounced off the second wall, and then, in quick succession, they heard it twice more, "HELLO….. HELLO."

"Let me have a go," shouted Mitch excitedly. "I'M MITCH!" he roared. Immediately, there came back the echo from the first wall, "I'M MITCH!" Then from the next wall came the same words, "I'M MITCH!" Next, they heard the sound again, "I'M

MITCH!" Then from the fourth wall they heard, "HELLO."

There was a stunned silence. Then Perry said, "What was that? The echo didn't sound quite right."

All four of them turned to face the fourth wall. "What happened?" asked Titch.

"I think the echoes got mixed up," said Mitch, in a small, quivering voice. "Perhaps we should go home. I don't think I want to spend the night here after all."

"Nonsense!" said Wiffen. "Somebody is having a joke with us. Let's find out who it is. Follow me." He then flapped his wings and raced over to the fourth wall as fast as he could. Reluctantly, the others followed him and they paced to and fro in front of the wall for ages. There was no rock they did not look behind. There was no cave where a person could hide. In fact, there was no hiding place anywhere.

"The echoes must have got mixed up," said Titch. "It's no big deal. I got five echoes and Mitch got three. Probably happens all the time."

Wiffen huffed and snorted. He wandered off on his own muttering, "It's a mystery and I don't like a mystery."

"Come on," said Titch, "let's try again."

Returning to the castle, they stood outside and this time Perry gave a huge bark. "WOOF, WOOF." Immediately, the huge 'WOOF' bounced off the walls and they heard it four times, loud and clear.

"It's back to normal now," said Mitch. "Anyway,

I'm hungry. Is it time for tea?"

Everyone agreed it was time for tea, so they all trooped into the castle, selected a room with a roof on, and settled down for their evening meal.

After they had eaten, they explored the quarry in great detail, satisfied themselves there was nobody else there, and settled down to spend the evening in

the castle. Titch and Mitch built a fire just outside the walls and soon they where singing songs and having a most enjoyable time.

As it got dark, they noticed a few drops of rain were falling and very soon it started to get very wet

indeed. The fire suddenly
started to hiss and steam
and soon it went out,
leaving the castle
quite dark. From his
hat, Mitch took his
magic feather, and
waved it over his
head. Immediately,
they could all see
again.

"Great," said
Perry, "Now
perhaps we had
better settle down
for the night
inside the castle
and get out of this
rain."

He was quite right,
because the rain was coming down quite heavily and
they were all getting extremely wet.

Soon they were settled in a large stone room
listening to the rain beating down on the new roof.

"What a nuisance," said Wiffen, in an irritated
voice. "Nobody will come and finish building the

castle in this weather. We're just wasting our time."

As he spoke, there came a loud rumbling noise in the distance, followed seconds later by a bright flash of lightning.

"Oh no, it's a thunderstorm," cried Mitch. "I hate thunderstorms!"

"Don't be a baby," said Wiffen, with no sympathy at all. "We are quite safe in this castle, and now there's a roof on, we won't get wet."

Another flash of lightning, which came with a huge crash of thunder, lit up the room so brightly that Mitch thought his feather was blazing of it's own accord.

"Just look at that storm," shouted Titch, who had climbed on to a stone table and was peering out of an open window. "It's just brilliant. I love thunderstorms! Come and look."

They all clambered on to the table to get a better view, apart from Mitch, who crawled underneath, and sat there quaking.

The storm got bigger and bigger and soon a wind got up that was so strong the whole castle started to shake. Great stones rolled and rattled against each other and horrid grinding noises came from every corner of the building. The shaking got worse and they all had to sit down to avoid falling off the table.

"The castle is going to fall down," cried Wiffen. "Quick. Let's get out of here!" They scrambled to the edge of the table, but it was shaking so much they couldn't climb down. "The window," shouted Wiffen.

"We can escape through the window."

Titch was first to reach the window, but he suddenly stopped, held out his arms and screamed, "GIANTS! Great, stone giants, and they're coming for us. Look!"

Wiffen and Perry joined him at the window, and they all started screaming, howling, barking, and jumping up and down at the same time. There, lumbering towards them, were four towering giants made entirely out of stone. They had long, stone arms and legs and great boulders for a body. On top of the body, they had heads made out of large, round rocks, with two red, gleaming eyes in each craggy face.

The only escape from the shaking castle led right

into the giants path. As the friends watched with horror, the four giants reached the castle and positioned themselves each beside a turret. Then, they stretched out their long, craggy arms, and joined their hands together so that they formed a circle that hugged the castle. As soon as they held the castle close to them, it stopped shaking, and although the storm raged all around, they remained firm and steady throughout.

Finally, the storm subsided, and the friends watched as the giants let go of the castle and sat wearily on the ground. By now, it was morning and in the early daylight, the giants could see that the castle was still standing and all the stones were still in place.

"What a narrow escape," said Titch. "It's a good job those giants came along, otherwise we would have been squashed under all the rocks when the castle fell down."

"They must be friendly giants after all," said Mitch.

"Yes, indeed!" cried Wiffen triumphantly, "And now we now who built the castle in the first place."

They all peered out of the window again, and Titch called out to the giants, "Thank you giants, you stopped the castle from falling down."

The nearest stone giant crouched down in front

of the window, and his rough-hewn face cracked as he smiled. When he spoke, his voice sounded like the low rumbling of distant thunder. "You're very welcome," he said. "However, it is *our* castle, and we didn't want it to fall down."

The other three giants joined the first one. One of them spoke in a similar rumbling voice, "You are our very first visitors, but aren't you tiny people!"

He looked closely at Wiffen and added, "Are you a bird? I've never seen a little, fat bird before. Can you fly?"

A very indignant Wiffen plumped up all the feathers from his wing tip to his tail and said, in a haughty manner, "Of course I'm a bird! I'm a very intelligent turkey and I can fly if I want to, but at the moment I don't want to."

"Who are you and where do you live?" asked Mitch, curious.

"My name is Rocky," rumbled the first giant. "Let me introduce my friends." He pointed a long, stony finger at one of the giants. "This is Granite." Then,

trying to whisper, he rumbled gently, "Don't call him
Granny, he doesn't like it." Pointing to the next
giant, he continued, "This is Slate. And the baby
giant next to him is called Pebble." This giant was
slightly smaller than the others, and as the friends
stared at him, he bowed politely.

The friends introduced themselves, and then
Wiffen asked, "Where do you live? We have searched
everywhere to find out who was responsible for
building this castle."

The four giants laughed together, and it sounded
like a volcano exploding. Then, Pebble explained,
"You could never find us, because we are part of the
quarry. We just melt into the walls, and if we don't

move, nobody knows we are there."

Granite joined in. "But we don't like getting wet, so we built this castle to shelter us."

"And," added Slate, "if anybody looks inside the castle when we are there, all they'll see is a pile of stones. That is, so long as we don't move."

They all laughed so much that the castle started to shake again.

"We must finish building the castle," rumbled Rocky. "I think we need a bit more weight on the roof."

"The echoes," said Titch, suddenly. "Are you responsible for the echoes in the quarry?"

"Oh yes, we have a lot of fun with the echoes," said Slate. "Only this time Pebble was very naughty."

Three of the giants turned to glare at Pebble, who looked a bit embarrassed. "I'm sorry," he said. "I just couldn't resist saying 'HELLO', instead of 'I'M MITCH'. I nearly split my sides laughing when the little, fat turkey flapped over and glared at me. I don't know how I kept a straight face."

They all laughed, except for Wiffen, who didn't like being called little, or fat, even if it was true. So he just glared at everybody and that made them all laugh even louder.

The four giants started to make the castle a bit

stronger by bringing in more stones from around the quarry, so the four friends decided it was time for them to go home.

But, before they went, Titch called out in a loud voice, "Hey giants, will you show us how you disappear?"

"Of course we will, and we will also show you how good we are at making echoes."

Each of the stone giants went to a different wall and simply stood against it. After a bit of a wiggle, they stood absolutely still and became part of the wall. The friends looked as hard as they could, but they could not see where the giants where standing."

"Oh my goodness," said Perry, quite astonished. "Isn't that clever?"

The two pixies said goodbye by roaring as loud as they could. "GOODBYE ROCKY, GRANITE, SLATE AND PEBBLE."

The reply bounced off the four walls in quick succession, "TITCH - MITCH - WIFFEN - PERRY."

The four friends climbed the path out of the

quarry, and just as they reached the top, they heard all four walls shout out together, "COME AGAIN SOON."

"We certainly will," said Wiffen. "Now we've solved the mystery of Echo Quarry."

5

The flying Carpet

THE HIGHEST POINT ON THE ISLAND WAS
called Bushy Hill and the only plum tree on the island
grew there. It supplied Titch and Mitch with the sweet
and tasty plums they loved to have with their tea.

One day they arrived at the top of the hill on their
magic bicycle to collect some plums, when suddenly
there was a whooshing noise and a shadow passed over
them. Looking up, they saw a carpet flying through the
air. It travelled away from them for a short distance
then suddenly it turned round and came racing back
at them. There was no time to study the strange flying
thing because it charged straight at them, and they
had to throw themselves to the ground to avoid being

knocked over. This time they
heard a voice call out, "Yahoo,
silly pixies! All pixies are
nincompoops!"

Looking up in amazement,
they saw the carpet hovering a
few metres away and leaning
out over the side was the head of a dark-coloured,
young gnome. As they watched, the gnome stuck out
his tongue and shouted, "Nobody likes pixies, they are
all horrid creatures!" Then, they heard the sound of
laughing as the gnome threw himself on his back and
kicked his legs in the air.

Titch and Mitch raced over to where the carpet

hovered, but it was just out of reach, even when they stretched their arms and jumped as high as they could. Once again, the head poked over the edge and looked down at them. It was a very cheeky looking gnome whose face grinned from ear to ear as he peered at them.

"Ha, ha," he said. "You can't catch me, I've got a flying carpet."

The two pixies looked at each other and Mitch said, "Oh yes we can!" They raced over to their magic bicycle and together called out the magic words, "Up, up and away!"

Immediately, the bicycle shot up into the air and, with Titch steering and Mitch hanging on behind him, they flew higher than the cheeky gnome. He looked up in surprise as, turning to face him, the bicycle and its two riders zoomed down towards him.

The bicycle came so fast, they nearly collided, but Titch skilfully swerved to one side just in time. As they passed by, Mitch reached down and grabbed the pointed hat from the startled gnome's head. With a great shriek, the new arrival fell off his carpet and landed on the ground with a bump. Without the gnome to control it, the carpet gave out a long hissing noise and dropped down on top of the gnome, covering him completely.

"Oh dear," said Titch, "I do hope he isn't hurt."

The two landed their bicycle and with great concern ran towards the struggling figure. They arrived in time to pull the carpet off the poor, spluttering fellow, who promptly sat up and beamed at them with his broad, impish grin.

"Brilliant!" he laughed, jumping to his feet and dusting himself down. "A flying bicycle. I never knew bicycles could fly. How absolutely marvellous!"

"Who are you?" asked Mitch, much relieved to find the gnome wasn't hurt, but still miffed at being dive-bombed by a carpet. When the gnome stood up to his full height, they found he was nearly as tall as them.

"I," he said grandly, placing one hand on his chest and sweeping the other before him, "am Ali Bong, son of Father Bong, and native of Sinbad City in Arabia."

"Why did you attack us?" asked Titch.

"I didn't attack you," said Ali indignantly. "I was just having some fun. After all, I haven't seen a pixie for ages. By the way, I like your magic bicycle. Please take me for a ride."

Ali gave them such a big, broad smile, that Titch found himself warming to the cheeky young gnome. Mitch, however, frowned deeply, refusing to be entranced by the little fellow's easy charm. After some small consideration, Titch said, "All right, you sit on the back and I'll show you how much better it is than that dusty old rug. I'll bet you fall off that thing a lot; it's got no seat and nothing to hold on to."

"Only when I hover around," replied Ali Bong, as he climbed up behind Titch. "It's fine for long distances."

With a cry of 'Up, up and away!', Titch pedalled a few times to move the bicycle forward, then, pulling back on the handlebars, he flew straight up into the air. Ali nearly fell off with surprise and, clutching Titch firmly round the waist, he shrieked with delight, "Fabulous! I love it."

"Don't show off!" shouted Mitch from below, unhappy at seeing his place taken by this little upstart. But it was no use. Titch turned a complete somersault at high speed, then turned and zoomed towards 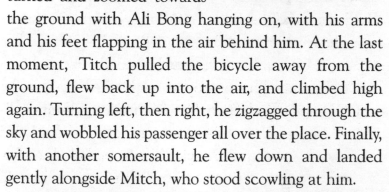 the ground with Ali Bong hanging on, with his arms and his feet flapping in the air behind him. At the last moment, Titch pulled the bicycle away from the ground, flew back up into the air, and climbed high again. Turning left, then right, he zigzagged through the sky and wobbled his passenger all over the place. Finally, with another somersault, he flew down and landed gently alongside Mitch, who stood scowling at him.

"That was brilliant!" Ali shouted as they landed. "I want one."

"Well, you can't have this one," said Mitch. "Anyway, you've got your carpet. Isn't that good enough?"

"Why don't you see for yourselves?" suggested Ali Bong, smiling.

"I don't think..." Mitch began, but before he could even finish his sentence, Titch jumped at the chance.

"I'd love a go," he cried, with great enthusiasm.

"Just step on it, and I'll make it take you for the ride of your lives." Ali walked onto the carpet and gestured with open hands for them to join him.

Titch stepped eagerly onto the carpet, then motioned to his brother to join him.

"I'm not so sure this is a good idea," said Mitch, folding his arms.

"Come on," implored Titch. "What's the harm? It'll be fun."

"Ever such fun," added Ali Bong, giving another of his wide grins.

Reluctant, and still frowning, Mitch followed his brother onto the carpet. It was bright red in colour with a blue star in the centre and intricate patterns all around the edge. At each end was a fringe of golden thread that sparkled in the sunlight.

"Sit down, my friends. Please sit down," encouraged Ali, gesturing them to take their place.

They did so, and found it was very fluffy and comfortable. "I'd still be afraid of falling off," said Titch. "What do we hold on to?"

"You'll be fine," said Ali smirking and, pressing the palms of his hands together, he bowed slightly and shuffled backwards off the carpet.

"You know, I really don't want to fly anywhere on

this," said Mitch anxiously, and was about to get off when Ali stood up straight, smirked again and, muttering something in a language neither of them understood, clapped his hands. Then, crying out in a loud voice, he said, "Carpet, go back to Sinbad City, NOW!"

Immediately the carpet shook itself so that the two pixies fell over with a bump. It then rolled itself up, trapping Titch and Mitch inside. The ends of the carpet closed together and it started to shake again. The two pixies howled in dismay and shouted, "Let us out, you wicked gnome!"

From inside their

prison they heard the gnome shout, "Hurrah, I've got a magic bicycle. Goodbye pixies!"

There was no escape. The carpet took off into the air and, with a little wiggle, zoomed higher and higher then set off at enormous speed towards the horizon.

Inside the rolled up carpet, the two pixies were actually quite comfortable, if a bit squashed, and they soon discovered they could look out of the small hole at the end and see the ground below. It was amazing how fast the carpet was flying. It was many times faster than their bicycle and the sheer speed took their breath away. Finally, they were going so fast they could no longer speak at all.

Eventually the carpet began to slow down and lose height. Looking out of the little hole, they found the land beneath them to be covered entirely in sand, stretching as far as the eye could see. After a short while, some buildings came into view. They saw a large, glittering palace surrounded by many small houses and domed buildings, with tall palm trees growing amongst them.

The carpet neared the palace, turned, then landed on the wide, stone steps. As it unrolled itself, Titch and Mitch sat up and found they were surrounded by a bustling crowd of very excited gnomes, all dressed in long white robes and red turbans. The gnomes examined them with curious expressions and muttered amongst themselves. Others were pointing at the carpet and talking in urgent voices. The two brothers felt quite embarrassed sitting there, lost and bewildered. As they stood up, their legs felt weak and shaky from being wrapped up in the blanket for so long.

At the bottom of the palace steps was a market square full of stalls selling food and clothes and jars and spices and all manner of exotic goods. It was up these steps that another gnome came running, waving a large poster in his hands and gesticulating wildly. He pushed through the crowd, showing everyone the poster. Voices began to rise. Reaching the front of the crowd, the gnome thrust the poster at the two pixies.

"STOLEN!" it read, in large black letters, "THE GRAND VIZIER'S CARPET. REWARD OFFERED!"

There was also a picture of the carpet, added for identification purposes. It was red with a blue star, exactly like the one they were standing on.

"Oh dear," said Titch. "It seems we're standing on stolen property. What are we going to do?"

Before Mitch could even reply, there was a commotion in the crowd, followed by the appearance of two soldiers in smart, red uniforms. They had small black beards, large moustaches, and wore white turbans on their heads. Each carried a long staff with a very large and quite sharp looking blade at the end.

"RUN!" screeched Mitch and he raced away from the soldiers, diving head first into the crowd and scrambling away on all fours. But Titch was too slow.

"We've got you, thief!" shouted the soldiers and, grabbing Titch by the scruff of the neck, dragged him away through the crowd.

Mitch heard Titch cry out and immediately stopped running. Turning around, he saw the two soldiers dragging Titch away towards the palace gates, so he ran back the way he had come. Keeping his head low, he followed them as best he could. But, since he

looked nothing like a gnome, least of all a gnome of the desert, he knew he could not stay hidden for long without being spotted.

Ducking into a side alley, Mitch found some washing hanging from a line under a window. One of the items on the line was a large, white cotton sheet. He grabbed this and, wrapping it about him, stepped back into the crowd trying his best to blend in and keep track of Titch.

When he next saw him, the soldiers were dragging Titch through some huge wooden doors into the centre of the palace compound. On the other side, behind high stone walls, stood a high tower, topped by

a massive golden dome shaped like an onion. The tower was the home of the Sultan. Built into the walls around it were windows and balconies supported by pillars, where gnomes waved down to friends in the street. Lots of other gnomes scurried to and fro, bustling in and out of the many doors, carrying bundles of paper or boxes stuffed with more paper. They all looked very busy.

The soldiers dragged a protesting Titch past a door with a sign that read, 'MINISTRY OF HOUSING', then another which read, 'MINISTRY OF WEALTH'. The next door had a sign reading, 'MINISTRY OF JUSTICE – COURT ROOMS'. The soldiers turned into it and slammed the door shut behind them.

Mitch could not follow, so he ran round the building and came upon another sign that read, 'PUBLIC GALLERIES'. It pointed up some wooden stairs to a balcony on which a number of gnomes were standing and looking through a window. Joining them,

he also looked inside and found that the court was in session. A judge sat at a long bench while prisoners were led out before him. The judge had a big, purple robe around his shoulders and, together with his beard and turban, looked to be a very stern judge indeed.

While Mitch was watching, a scruffy little gnome was brought before the judge, who leaned back in his chair and banged a hammer on the table in front of him. "What has this wretch done?" demanded the judge in a deep voice.

"He broke a window while playing football," came the reply.

"Guilty," snapped the judge. "He can spend a week in the mouse hole." A soldier stepped forward carrying a small pot of lurid, green powder and sprinkled a generous pinch of it over the naughty gnome. Mitch watched in amazement as the gnome suddenly shrank down to the size of a mouse, was picked up by the soldier and carried across the courtroom towards a small door in the wall. Opening the door, the soldier thrust the miniature gnome into a tiny hole in the wall, where he disappeared at once with a fearful squeak. All the gnomes around Mitch cheered and laughed as the soldier then slammed the door shut.

Mitch turned to the watching crowd and said in surprise, "What happened?"

An old lady gnome next to him cackled and said, "That's shrinking powder. All the jails in Sinbad City are full, so the judge makes all the prisoners shrink so they can fit inside small cages in the mouse hole. That teaches them not to be naughty! Ha, ha, ha."

Mitch returned to the window and, to his horror, he saw Titch brought out before the judge.

"What has this wretch done?"

"He stole a flying carpet."

"You have a shifty look about you pixie. Guilty!" roared the judge. "Six months in the mouse hole."

"But I didn't steal anything!" protested Titch. But it was to no avail. The soldier with the pot of shrinking powder stepped forward and tossed a handful over the distraught pixie. To Mitch's horror, he saw Titch shrink down to the size of a small mouse. Immediately, the soldier grabbed the tiny Titch and, although he struggled and squealed, pushed him down the mouse hole out of sight and the door slammed shut behind him.

As Mitch stood staring in through the window wondering what to do next, he failed to notice that his bedsheet had slipped down to his shoulders, revealing his very ungnome-like face. A guard standing nearby spotted him and called out, "That's the other thieving pixie! Detain him!"

Before anyone could get a hand to him, Mitch bounded down the steps, jumped to the ground and fled. He dashed past startled gnomes who joined the guards in the chase, shouting as they ran: "Stop thief! Stop thief!"

Turning a corner, Mitch crashed into a market stall, knocking over some baskets full of oranges and pears, which spilled across the path behind him. Some gnomes stopped to pick up the tumbling produce, causing the guards and the rest of the chasing gnomes to crash into them. Everyone fell over and others tripped over them as well, and soon there was a great mass of crumpled gnomes splayed on the floor and writhing in squashed fruit.

By the time Mitch had turned three more corners, he found there was nobody behind him giving chase. He had escaped.

He stopped to get his breath back. Then, turning another corner, found himself back in the market place. Pulling the bedsheet tightly around him, he wandered aimlessly, trying to think clearly, when he recalled the words Ali Bong had used when he introduced himself: "I am Ali Bong, the son of Father Bong." If I can find Father Bong, thought Mitch, he might be able to help.

The very first gnome that Mitch asked said, "Oh yes, everybody knows Father Bong. He runs the pharmacy just around the corner."

Following the directions given to him, Mitch soon found the shop and walked boldly inside. It was a cramped, dusty shop, with shelves on every wall reaching right up to the ceiling. On the shelves were bottles and jars of exotic medicines and mysterious potions. Behind a high, wooden counter, stood a

crooked old man, busily mixing powders in a small metal bowl and muttering to himself in a very agitated fashion. He had tiny reading glasses perched on his thin nose, watery blue eyes and a long, pointed, white beard.

Mitch cleared his throat. "Excuse me," he said.

"What is it?" said the old man. "Can't you see I'm busy?" He looked to one side, flipped over a page of a very old book that stood propped up beside him, and began to study it minutely.

"I'm looking for the father of Ali Bong," said Mitch, and sneezed. The dust was beginning to bother him.

"Then you've found him," said the old man sharply and, looking up at Mitch, raised his eyebrows at the sight of Mitch's curious disguise. "We don't get many pixies in here."

Mitch blew his nose on the sheet.

"Have you news of my son?" asked Father Bong, adjusting his spectacles.

Mitch came straight to the point. "Your son Ali landed his flying carpet on our island, then tricked us into bringing it back here to Sinbad City so he could steal our bicycle! Is he always so naughty?"

The old man held up his hands in surprise and gasped in astonishment. "Oh my goodness! Whatever next? Is he all right?"

"He's fine, sadly, but I am very unhappy and my

brother Titch is in the mouse hole prison."

"Please tell me everything," said Father Bong with a resigned sigh and, coming out from behind the counter, offered Mitch a chair.

Titch told the old man the whole story. He listened intently, nodding all the while and occasionally letting out a long, sad sigh.

"Well you did the right thing in coming to see me," he said, when Mitch had finished his sorry tale. "The carpet belongs to the Grand Vizier and I was putting some magic back into it when it was stolen. Luckily, my assistant found it on the palace steps this afternoon and brought it back."

Moving in the back of the shop, Mitch could see the gnome who had run up the steps waving the poster.

"That's your assistant, is it?" he said angrily. "Well, he has got my brother and me into big trouble."

"He's a hard worker," the old man replied. "And the Grand Vizier is a very stern man. If he found out I'd lost his carpet, he'd have my head in return."

The old man turned away shaking his fist.

"I should have known Ali had taken it. How many times must I tell that boy..?" He turned to Mitch with a renewed sense of urgency in his voice.

"We must do something to get him home. Where did you say this island of yours is?"

"We have to get Titch out of prison first," said Mitch firmly.

"Of course, of course," said Father Bong. "I couldn't agree more. Let me think for a minute now."

He turned away again, scratching his chin and muttering under his breath.

"I know what we can do," he said at last, thrusting a triumphant finger in the air. "Once your brother is free, I will give the carpet strict instructions. First, it is to take you back to your island, and then you must try to find Ali. It should not be too difficult, he usually leaves a trail of devastation and mischief wherever he goes. You need to get him onto the carpet, stand well back, and watch the carpet follow its instructions. He will then no longer be a problem for you. I promise this with all my heart."

"I hope you do," replied Mitch, sternly. "But how do we free my brother?"

"Yes, yes! Now, it so happens that I provide the courts with the shrinking powder."

"You make that stuff?" gasped Mitch in surprise.

"Yes. Very good, isn't it? I'm rather proud of it myself. Of course I also make the growing powder that turns released prisoners back into their former selves. Can't have one without the other now, can we? Now, listen to me, this is what you must do. First, we shall dress you up as an old woman with a basket of food."

"An old woman?" cried Mitch, quite astonished. "Why an old woman?"

"It's better than a bedsheet. Now pay attention," said Father Bong firmly. "All will be revealed…"

A short while later, towards tea time, an old lady gnome, all bent and shuffling, knocked on the back door of the mouse hole prison. The jailers let her in and waved her towards the cages where the tiny, shrunken prisoners where held.

Mitch, playing his part well, shuffled along the narrow corridor, past cage after cage, inside each of which sat or stood or lay a very small prisoner. All the shrunken gnomes looked very miserable indeed. At

each cage, Mitch would deposit a few crumbs of food onto a plate and then move on. Knowing he was being watched, he had  to be very careful not to attract too much attention.

He came to one cage and inside spotted the scruffy, window-breaking gnome, who simply glared at him but said nothing. After passing along a few more cages, Mitch finally spotted Titch, right at the end of the

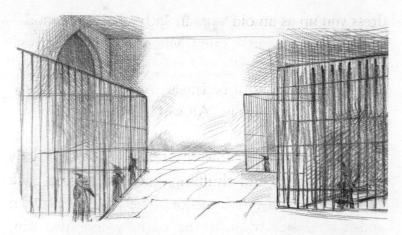

line, slumped against the bars and looking even more miserable than the rest of the prisoners. Looking back at the jailers, Mitch saw they had lost interest in him and were talking amongst themselves.

"Psst," he said to Titch, who looked up, his face brightening immediately at the sight of his brother. Carefully, Mitch slid the catch on Titch's cage and, as

he reached in to place the food, signalled to the tiny Titch that he should climb up the sleeve of his robe, which he did without delay. Then he closed the cage, turned around and, with Titch nestled snugly in his armpit, shuffled towards the door. But as he passed the guards, they looked up, surprised by the sudden sound of a sneeze that came from under Mitch's cloak.

"Uh-oh," said Mitch, without thinking, and before he knew it, the game was up.

"Stop!" cried a guard, jumping to his feet, but Mitch chose to run instead. As he reached the door, he stopped, turned and faced the four guards that were coming towards him.

"What are you doing?" cried Titch, from inside his robe.

"Sit tight. Don't move!" Mitch answered and, reaching inside the basket, grabbed the package that

Father Bong had given him.

As the four guards got nearer, Mitch raised the package and flung it at them. The package burst, covering them in lurid, green powder. Immediately, the guards shrank to the size of mice, and ran around in circles on the floor.

Mitch darted out of the door and into the street. He made his way back to the shop of Father Bong and, staggering in through the door, he collapsed in a heap on the floor. From under his robe crawled out a scruffy and rather dizzy Titch. He looked up at Father Bong, then at Mitch, and started to shout, but all they could hear was a tiny squeak.

Father Bong had the growing powder ready and quickly sprinkled a tiny amount over Titch. It was a deep blue in colour, and the result was amazing. Titch started to grow very quickly, getting bigger and bigger, until he was back to his normal size.

"About time to," he said, dusting himself off. "I thought I was going to stay in that prison for ever. It's horrid, being so little. Well done Mitch, and thank you!"

"This is Father Bong," said Mitch by way of introduction.

"There's no time left,"

141

cried Father Bong. "The Grand Vizier will soon be here. He's heard about you too, and he wants his carpet back."

"What will you do?" asked Mitch, concerned for the old man's safety.

"Stall him," he said, and held up a small tub of dark red powder and showed it to them. "I have some stalling powder ready, just in case. Now then, quickly does it, out into the back yard and onto the carpet."

They hurried outside and could already hear a troop of guards marching down the street. The pixies jumped onto the carpet.

"Goodbye," said Father Bong, waving his hand. "Have a safe trip and don't forget to follow my instructions. I must have that carpet back by tonight." Then he said a few words in a strange tongue. Immediately, the carpet shook itself so that the pixies fell down. Then it rolled itself up in the same way that it had done before and, after a few moments hovering in the air just above the shop, it zoomed off at high speed back across the desert. This time it flew even faster than when it had brought them to Sinbad City, and before long they felt it slowing down until, with a gentle bump, it landed and unrolled itself.

Titch and Mitch where startled to find it had landed in their own garden. They also found themselves in the middle of a rainstorm, with huge drops landing all around them.

"Oh, what a nuisance," cried Mitch. "We'll have to search for that Ali Bong in the rain!"

"No, the rain is a good thing," responded Titch. "It means that our magic bicycle won't fly, so wherever that mischievous little Ali Bong is, you can be sure he'll be grounded."

Just at that moment Budgie landed beside them, shook all her feathers to get rid of the rain and said, "I say you two, why have you left your bicycle on the beach? That's no way to treat a thing like that."

"On the beach!" they shouted together. "Hurrah! Well done Budgie."

Without another word, they picked up the carpet, raced across the meadow and ran down the winding path to the beach. There, sitting in a cave, with his elbows on his knees, his head resting in his hands and looking thoroughly miserable, was Ali Bong.

"There you are," cried Mitch. "You haven't gone very far, have you?"

Ali looked up at them and said, gloomily, "It's a

horrid bike after all. It doesn't like the rain and I can tell it doesn't like me. I want my carpet back."

Titch and Mitch rolled out the carpet and Ali cheered up straight away. "Super-duper! Now I can explore the world again."

"Check it out," said Mitch, "you must make sure we haven't damaged it in any way."

The two pixies watched as Ali jumped onto the carpet. However, it had been given secret instructions and, as soon as Ali's feet touched it, the carpet gave a hefty shake. The young gnome fell over, and the carpet rolled itself up with Ali Bong inside. With a final wiggle, it rose into the air and whizzed higher and higher, until finally it vanished over the horizon.

"What a day!" said Mitch. "I never want to see another flying carpet as long as I live."

"And what's more," added Titch, "We still haven't got any plums for our tea!"